humphrey's bear

By Jan Wahl ∼ Illustrated by William Joyce

Henry Holt and Company ∼ New York

Henry Holt and Company, LLC
Publishers since 1866
115 West 18th Street
New York, New York 10011
www.henryholt.com

Library of Congress Cataloging-in-Publication Data
Wahl, Jan.
Humphrey's bear.
Summary: Humphrey has wonderful adventures with his toy bear
after they go to bed at night, just as his father did before him.
1. Children's stories, American.   [1. Bedtime—Fiction.
2. Bears—Fiction.] I. Joyce, William, ill. II. Title.
PZ7.W1266Hu   1987   [E]   85-5541

ISBN-13: 978-0-8050-7812-1 / ISBN-10: 0-8050-7812-6 (hardcover)
1 3 5 7 9 11 13 15 14 12 10 8 6 4 2
ISBN-13: 978-0-8050-7887-9 / ISBN-10: 0-8050-7887-8 (paperback)
1 3 5 7 9 11 13 15 14 12 10 8 6 4 2

First published in hardcover in 1987 by Henry Holt and Company
First paperback edition, 1989
Revised, redesigned hardcover and paperback editions, 2005
Printed in China

For Indivar Augustus Wahl,
also known as Indy-bear
—J. W.

For my lifelong pal
and confidante, Melissa
—W. J.

When Humphrey went up the stairs to bed, he heard his father say, "Isn't Humphrey too old to sleep with a toy bear?"

Humphrey didn't hear what his mom said.

He just jumped under the blanket, snuggled with the brown bear, and slept.

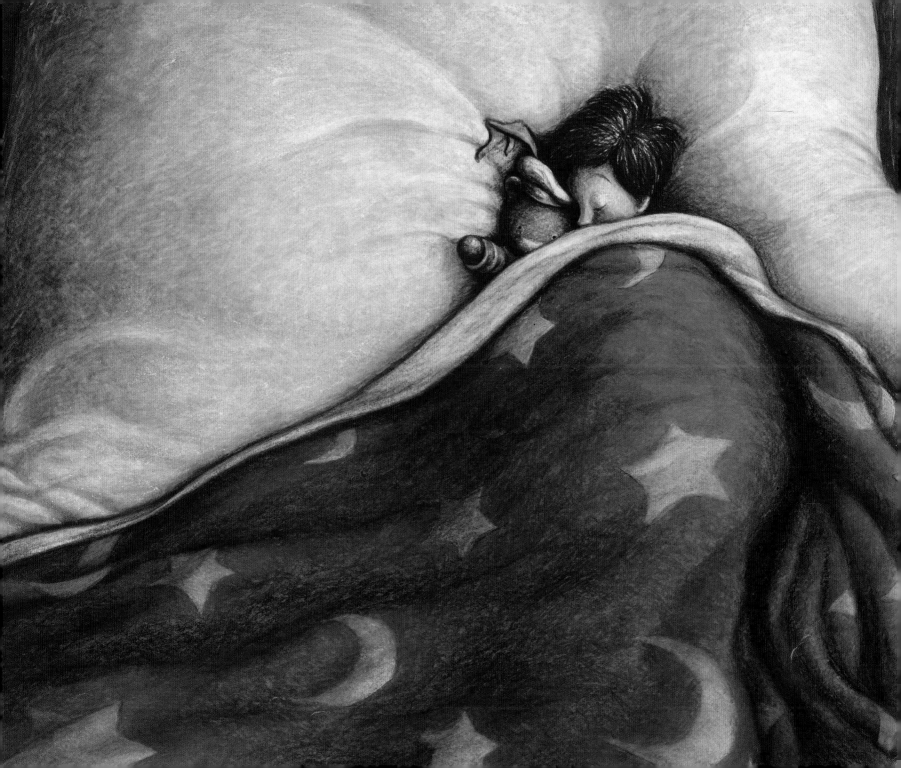

As soon as Humphrey was asleep,
the bear grew big, as it always did,
and took him by the hand.

"Get up!" called the bear, standing
in the moonlight. "Our boat is waiting.

Here is your cap. Let's go!"

Quietly, Humphrey followed the bear downstairs and out the kitchen door.

Now, there was a river running beyond the wet green night grass. At the end of long planks lay a sailboat.

"Take the helm. Steer!" shouted the bear, pulling the ropes of high-flying sails. "Cast off!"

They sailed right out of the backyard.

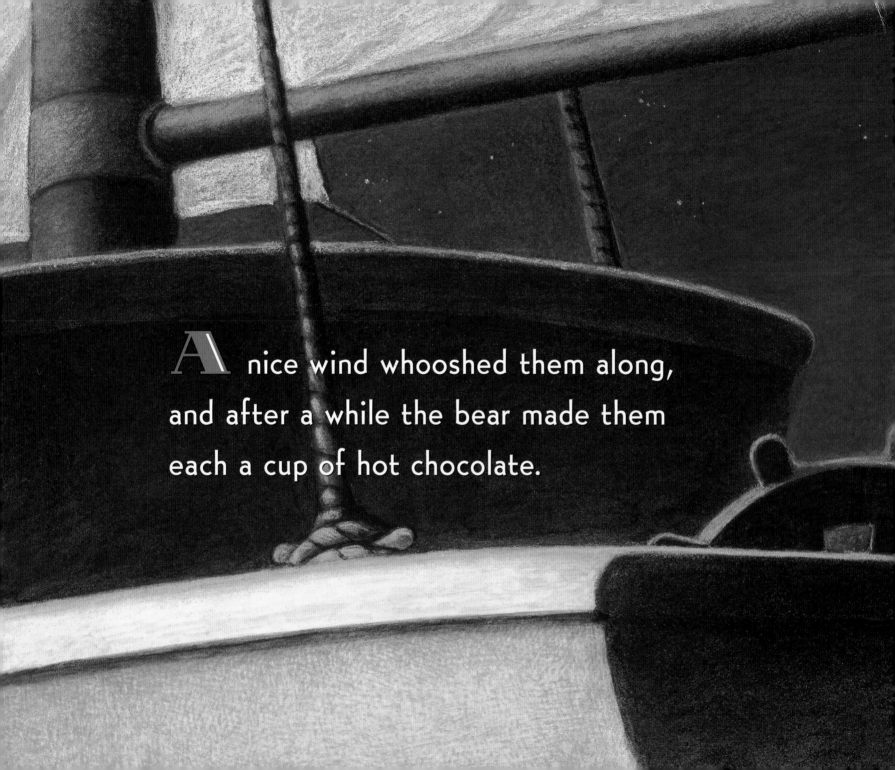

A nice wind whooshed them along, and after a while the bear made them each a cup of hot chocolate.

Soon the river flowed into a huge wet sea, and porpoises sang sea songs. Humphrey steered by the stars, while the shaggy bear danced.

Suddenly, a typhoon came up, and
the bear slipped and fell off the deck.
Humphrey dived for his friend.
"Where are you?" said Humphrey.
"Blub, blub!" said the bear.

I will *save* you!" yelled Humphrey.
But he could not find the bear, though
he swam and he swam and he swam . . .

. . . until he came to an island.

Over a sandy hill he heard a dreamy banjo playing. And who do you think was playing that banjo?

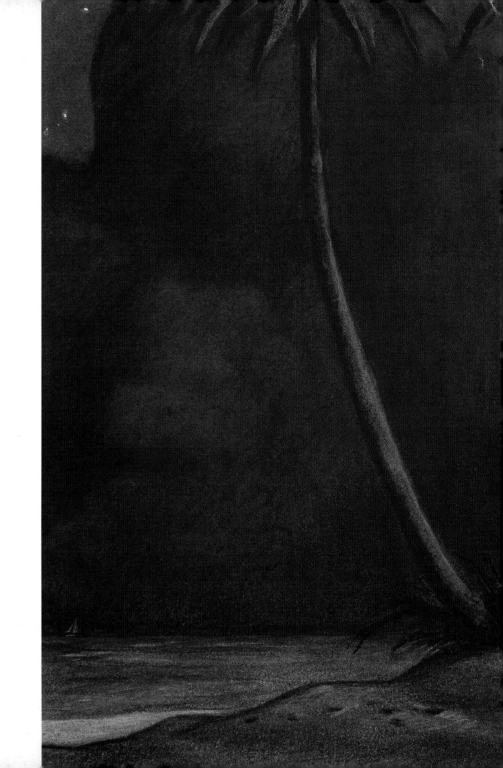

Humphrey found the bear, and the moon outside and the hot chocolate inside warmed them.

Humphrey could smell the bear's wonderful furry fur. They shut their eyes, and the next thing Humphrey knew . . .

. . . he was in bed.

"*Bear! Where ARE you?*" yelled Humphrey.

His father was holding the toy bear in the moonlight, remembering when that bear was *his* bear.

"Here, Son," he whispered.

Smiling, his father put the little
bear back in Humphrey's hands.
"I used to sail with him, too."